Tricks for Treats on Halloween

Tricks for Treats on Halloween

By Leonard Kessler

Drawings by Tom Eaton

GARRARD PUBLISHING COMPANY
CHAMPAIGN, ILLINOIS

Library of Congress Cataloging in Publication Data

Kessler, Leonard P. 1920-
Tricks for treats on Halloween.

SUMMARY: Strange things happen when a witch, a dragon, and a ghost go trick-or-treating.
[1. Halloween—Fiction] I. Eaton, Tom. II. Title.

PZ7.K484Tr [E] 78-21942
ISBN 0-8116-6075-3

Tricks for Treats on Halloween

Trick or treat!
It's Halloween!

Boo!

Boo to you!

Wait for me.

I want to go with you.

They went
down the street
to trick or treat.

Look, a ghost!

Look, a witch!

Look, a dragon!

Let's knock here.

Trick or treat!

Here are treats
for you.

Now
do a trick for us.

Wow!

How do you do that?

I'm a witch.
I do magic tricks.

Let's knock here.

Trick or treat!

Here are treats
for you.

Now
do a trick for us.

Wow!

How do you do that?

I'm a ghost.
I can fly.

Let's knock here.

Trick or treat!

Here are treats
for you.

Now
do a trick for us.

Wow!

How do you do that?

I'm a dragon.
I do magic tricks.

Now come to our house
for trick or treat.
You will have
apples and cookies
and other good things to eat.

Happy Halloween!